add vowels to the letters below?

mrvls

lghtr

rmbl

fr

Th Vwl Fml

Tl f Lst Lttrs

JST MRRD!

VWLS

Sll M. Wlkr   llstrtns b **Kvn Lthrdt**

Crlrhd Bks   Mnnpls · Nw Yrk

For Aisling Power and her siblings, Eoin (pronounced Owen), Ivan, Ursula, and Aidan—the original vowel family. Also for the readers at the Saint Charles (Illinois) Literature Festival, the place where this story was born.

—S.M.W.

To Grandpa Luthardt and Grandpa Walt. In loving memory of Grandma Luthardt and Grandma Mancil. Thank you, Jesus!

—K.L.

Text copyright © 2008 by Sally M. Walker
Illustrations copyright © 2008 by Kevin Luthardt

Carolrhoda Books
A division of Lerner Publishing Group, Inc.
241 First Avenue North
Minneapolis, MN 55401 U.S.A.

Website address: www.lernerbooks.com

Library of Congress Cataloging-in-Publication Data

Walker, Sally M.
    The Vowel family: a tale of lost letters / by Sally M. Walker ; illustrated by Kevin Luthardt.
        p.   cm.
    Summary: The members of the Vowel family have a hard time talking until their children, Alan, Ellen, Iris, Otto, and Ursula, are born, and when one of them gets lost one day, it takes their Aunt Cyndy to fix the problem.
    ISBN 978-0-8225-7982-3 (lib. bdg. : alk. paper) [1. Vowels—Fiction. 2. Humorous stories.] I. Luthardt, Kevin, ill. II. Title.
    PZ7.W153845Me 2008
    [Fic]—dc22   2007009952

Manufactured in the United States of America
1 2 3 4 5 6 — JR — 13 12 11 10 09 08

Whn Pm Smth mrrd Sm Vwl, sh sd, "Lf s wndrfl!"
"xcpt whn w tlk," Sm sd. "Tlkng s vr hrd."

ftr **Alan** and **Ellen**, the twns, were brn,
ther parents gggled wth glee. Alan
and Ellen's clear speech made sense.

At schl, when the teacher asked Alan's name, he stated, "Call me Alan Vwel."

Lfe was better. Bt t wasn't perfect.

"r faml lacks zest," declared Alan and Ellen.
"Papa and Mama, we want pets."

"We'll get a cat and an ape!" answered Sam.

"And an elephant and an egret!" added Pam.

Grwng chldren need vegetables and gd fd. Sam was a master chef.

"Dad prepares delectable breakfasts!" Alan declared.

"Let's have pancakes and scrambled eggs," added Ellen.

"Nt ths mrnng. We have n eggs. r flr and btter are gne," Pam answered.

"What?" asked Sam.

Gsh darn t. Ths jst sn't acceptable. Smethng's stll mssng!

Cndtns mprved after **Iris** and **Otto**,
another pair of twins, joined the famil.

At last, people comprehended when the Vowels said their names! Life became precise, even exceptional. Of course, Iris and Otto got pets too . . .

An insect
and an ibex.
An otter
and an okapi.

However, when Alan tried
to enter with a triceratops,
Sam stamped his foot.

Thank goodness **Ursula** chose
just that moment to be born!

Ursula—born speaking because miracles do occur—pronounced her first words with care.

Puffed with pride at his daughter's dialogue,
Sam hugged all of his children.

"Alan, Ellen, Iris, Otto, and Ursula. Our lives are complete."

"Not quite. We lack a duck and a unicorn. And a humongous house," Pam replied.

Since Pam was a master builder, the outrageous situation left her unruffled. "This calls for an excursion to the lumber store," she said.

LUMBER SHACK

SALE TODA

50% OFF
ALL LUMBER, ALL DA

Pam, Sam, and their quintet of
kids trooped downtown. Otto
trotted until his foot got sore.
The poor bo slowed to a stop.

When the famil reached the lumber stre, Pam realized tt was lst. She began t weep. Sam cried buckets. Ellen, Alan, and Ursula bawled till their peepers turned red.

Thank gdness fr Iris, a quick thinker. She whipped ut her cell phne and called Aunt Cyndy.

Aunt Cyndy was mre than family.
She was als chief f plice.

"Dry yur eyes," said Aunt Cyndy.
"Finding tt requires strategy, nt tears."

"This mystery," said Aunt Cyndy, "has me stymied."

Finally, she smiled. "tt and I are a lt alike. We bth lve a gd yarn."

"*YARN!*" they all yelled.

The family ran tward the Knitter's Shp.

The Vwels turned and stared.

"A 'yarn' is a synnym fr a gd stry," said Aunt Cyndy. "Climb in my van. I knw where we'll find tt."

"The library has great stries," said
Aunt Cyndy as they climbed the steps.
"And Mrs. Cliff has stry time right nw."

In the Children's Room, Otto and the other kids were hanging on Mrs. Cliff's words. As she turned the page, she smiled at the Vowels. "Please come join us as we begin chapter two."

READ

BALL

TRUCK

CHAPTER 2

After their eventful outing, the Vowels were glad to go home.

But the next time you visit the library, be sure to look for the Vowels. They go there often. Why?

Because **A**lan, **E**llen, **I**ris, **O**tto, **U**rsula, and *sometimes* Aunt C**y**ndy are always ready to be part of a good story.

What words can you make when you

A E

frm bngl cw mss zp